Gifts of the Magpie

by Sam Hundley

CAPSTONE EDITIONS
a capstone imprint

3907506934958

The magpie is good
at finding things.
She finds treasures
others have lost
or left behind.

One day she asked her friends,
"What can I find for you?"

The goat who was tired of winter replied,

"Spring!"

The lonely mouse replied,
"Another mouse."

"Click away!" said the magpie.

"Sigh . . . ," said the mouse.

The hog without
a home replied,

"A pen of my
very own!"

"Here you go, Shakespeare," said the magpie.

"Snort," said the hog.

The hungry squirrel replied,

"A nut would be nice."

"Nut-thing would make me happier!" said the magpie.

"Uh . . . ,"
said the squirrel.

The farsighted
owl replied,

"A pair of
glasses, please."

"Cheers!"
said the magpie.

"Not what I had in mind,"
said the owl.

The boy who loved
baseball replied,

"I could
use a bat."

"Catch!"
said the magpie.

"Help!" cried the boy.

The magpie meant well,
but she got everyone's
wishes **wrong.**

At first, her friends were disappointed.

But the more they thought about it,

the better each
gift became . . .

The goat bounced on the spring,
which warmed his heart . . .

The mouse went online and
connected with an old friend . . .

The hog used the pen
to sign a lease on a
cozy apartment
with a roof . . .

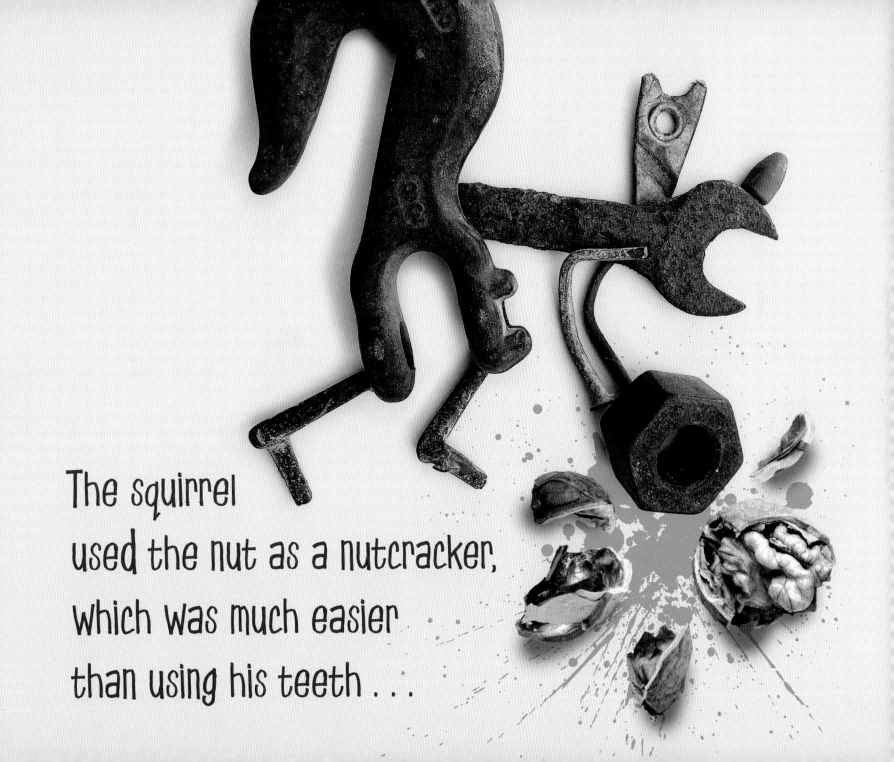

The squirrel
used the nut as a nutcracker,
which was much easier
than using his teeth . . .

The owl found that
she could see again
when looking through
the glasses . . .

And the boy had a pal
for playing catch!

"Hurray!" cheered her friends.

"AW, shucks,"
said the magpie.

Mistakes happen,

but creative thinking . . .

can turn blunders into

wonders!

About the Art

A lot of the objects used in creating the illustrations in this book are "dug relics"—old metal fragments from long ago that were unearthed by inquisitive treasure hunters using metal detectors and shovels. Two friends of mine in particular have generously donated a lot of these things to me, without which this book would not have been possible. Thank you, Roy Bahls and Vicky Friedrichs!

Can you identify some of the things that were used? The mouse's ears are made of flat buttons that are more than 100 years old. The magpie's tail feathers are made of blue-and-white pottery shards placed on a putty knife. Can you find these other objects?

- blue and black combs
- an old paintbrush
- a tarnished spoon
- a pair of metal snips

- a rusty wrench
- a tiny buckle
- a bullet for a nose
- buttons for eyes

Make your own scrap Art!

Create a work of art using found objects, then take a photo of it on a white background. (You don't have to glue everything down.) Send the photo to sam@samhundley.com. He'd love to see it!

Did you know?

Magpies are some of the most intelligent birds on Earth! They have approximately the same brain-to-body ratio as we humans do. Like their cousin the crow, magpies often decorate their nests with objects they collect. Unlike other birds, magpies can recognize themselves in a mirror. Magpies are good mimics and can imitate car alarms and barking dogs.

Homonyms are words that have the same spelling or pronunciation but different meanings. Several homonyms, such as "spring" and "bat," are used in this book. Can you think of any other homonyms? It's easy to see how the poor magpie misunderstood what her friends meant when the words they used have multiple meanings!

About the Artist

Sam Hundley is an American scrap artist. He creates folk art using found objects—all kinds of stuff from scrapyards, vacant lots, and along roadsides. "I love the look of rusty metal, flaking paint, and weathered wood," he says. "So, for many years, I just collected things like flattened aerosol cans and leather gloves until I had a big box full of junk. Then, in October 2009, I was inspired to create a series of trick-or-treaters out of these objects. Dracula, Abe Lincoln, a werewolf—they came out looking a lot like my drawings." Retired after 39 years as a newspaper artist (where he made a lot of mistakes!), Sam now resides in Norfolk, Virginia, with his wife, Lynndale, and their beagle, Theo.

Gifts of the Magpie is published by Capstone Editions, an imprint of Capstone.
1710 Roe Crest Drive
North Mankato, Minnesota 56003
www.capstonepub.com

Library of Congress Cataloging-in-Publication Data is available on the Library of Congress website.
ISBN: 978-1-6844-6214-8 (hardcover)
ISBN: 978-1-6844-6215-5 (ebook PDF)

Summary: A scrappy story with an excellent message, *Gifts of the Magpie* tells of a bighearted bird who loves to find things and loves to help—but confusion over homonyms causes the bird to get everything wrong! Will the magpie ever get it right? Then the bird's friends take a second look at the gifts and realize that, with a little creativity, the magpie gave them just what they needed. Scrap-illustrations provide a feast for the eyes, and young readers will delight in discovering how found objects can be transformed into treasures.

Editorial Credits:
Editor: Kristen Mohn; Designer: Bobbie Nuytten; Production Specialist: Kathy McColley

Author photo credit: Randall Greenwell

Design Element: Shutterstock: domnitsky, 23 (walnut)

This book is dedicated to my wife, Lynndale Hundley, for her enthusiastic support of my very messy art.

I'd also like to thank Krys Stefansky for her great suggestions and copy editing.

—S.H.

Printed and bound in China. 3741

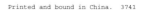